Purple Pennies

Tatiana Whigham

Published by Revival Waves of Glory Books & Publishing

PO Box 596| Litchfield, Illinois 62056 USA

www.revivalwavesofgloryministries.com

Revival Waves of Glory Books & Publishing is committed to excellence in the publishing industry.

Published in the United States of America

Paperback: 978-1-68411-175-6

Table of Contents

Chapter One

Geesh, it's almost half past six and Brian's still not here. We only have thirty minutes to get to the church, and traffic is going to be a mess. Peeking out of the window yet again, there's still no sign of him.

Taking a deep breath, I try my best to ease the situation by saying, "It's okay Trish. Just relax; he'll be here." Talking more to myself than anything, I mumble, "Uhhhh, the nerve of some men!" Of all of the nights, he had to pick tonight. He knows that tonight is our annual leadership conference. I've finally been promoted to Lead Evangelist of the Outreach ministries and I'm beyond excited. There were three candidates up for the job and the committee chose me; the only female in the bunch! Tell me that women aren't meant to lead. In all honesty, I had to sacrifice a lot to get this position. With all of the long hours, working on weekends, and all out constant devotion to the cause, I know that I've really put my marriage in a rut, but I mean, Brian should understand. Women sacrifice their dreams and goals for men all of the time. And with me being the breadwinner of the relationship, he's got to understand that I've been doing all this for us. I knew that he had a deep passion for automotive and mechanics when I married him three years ago, but let's face it, there's no way that we can live off of a $1,200 a month salary. With three fresh model cars, totaling up to $2,200 in car payments and car insurance along with this brand new mortgage (roughly totaling to about $1,800 a month), it's clear that I've been the one pulling the weight financially. But again, I knew that my job would have to carry the household. But lately Brian's been killing me with this I'm the head of the house crap. If you want to be the head of the house, then you first have to lead by example. I mean, I can't help the fact that I make over $200,000 a year as the District Manager for Barker's Reality. I started my path at the bottom of the ranks with no college degree and in as little as ten years, I've soared to the top in both the church and my career. If anything, he should be nothing but proud of me.

Checking the driveway again, still nothing. Jesus, how long does it take to go downtown and back? Glancing at the clock again, it's ten minutes 'til. "Why Brian, why?" as I crash on the nearest sofa. Maybe it's my fault. I probably should've told him about the job. But I know Brian; he'll only try to talk me out of it. I can hear him now ramping and raging, 'What about me? Where am I going to work?' Please, he's a mechanic, it's not like it's some hard trade. He can find work anywhere. This job has everything. I'd be a fool to turn it down. Not only is it more pay, but it's also the freedom to travel and evangelize all over the world for a whole year. My first assignment is to construct and carry out a two week tour of 'God's Path To Redemption' (which we do every year might I add) which spans across 12 cities and 6 states. And as an added bonus, I get the privilege to rebuild both a church and a community in Zimbabwe. Is that cool or what?

Looking at the clock again, it's now five minutes 'til. I might as well go ahead and call this fool for like the fifth time already. Hearing the dial tone on the end only irritates me even more. Just as I'm about to leave yet another hot voice message, I hear a key turn in the door way. It's about time.

"Brian!" I call out as I stroll down the hallway. "Brian, I know that you heard—"

Just as I reach the door way, I see it. Three men, one of which appears to be Brian. The other two look every bit of common hoodlums, one of which is holding a gun to Brian's head. Two seconds of this and it's clear to me that this is no game.

"Get on the ground lady. Now!" yells the shorter one of the two from what I can gather, but stunned and shocked, my feet refuse to move. At this point the horror calls my tears to focus, and at this point, my mind's no help. I can't tell A from Z right now.

"I said get down!" he snaps knocking me to the ground with one deadly blow to the head.

Cradling myself in pain, I feel my head as it throbs, only to see my hand return to me in trails of my own blood. Looking up in horror, I watch as the men push Brian down as well. One man locks the door, while the other drags us both (which even now, I don't see how) to the living room just a few feet away.

"Yo Kid, handle this while I do a quick walk through." yells the shorter one yet again. You know, if I was as spaciously challenged as he is, I would think twice about ordering somebody else around that's three times my height, but the other guy seems to follow just the same.

As I sneak a look at Brian, trying to find some sort of explanation for this mayhem, I find none. His eyes appear to be just as worried and confused as I am. That figures, when you need him to step up as a man, he's useless. So that leaves me looking around the room for something; anything to help us but all I see is the extension cord dangling from behind the couch. Well, that's going to have to do tonight.

"Hey, take this." says the shorter guy as he hands over a gun to the taller one.

"And don't let them out of your sight." Taking a second to let his words sink in, he continues, "I mean it man, don't do anything stupid."

"Alright."

"You got it."

"Dang man, I said alright. You just worry about you and hurry up. I don't want to be in this joint a minute longer than I have to."

Cracking a smile, the shorter one replies, "Yeah, alright." And with that, he heads up the staircase doing God knows what. With him out of the picture, it's clear that it's only me and the tall guy. Brian shouldn't even be counted; he's over here crying and squealing worse than I am. Using the face to face training that I've been learning in my leadership class, I know that the first step to knocking down the barrier of influence is to 'bring the battlefield to common ground.' You know, to talk on a level where the opposing person can both understand and reason with you. So putting my training into action, here I go.

"So, what's your name, Champ?"

He turns to me for the first time and actually looks into my eyes, it's clear that the mere fact of me talking scares the mess out of him. But looking around the room, he's not the only one scared out of his wits.

Brian cracks a look at me so hard that reads, 'What-In-God's-Name-Are-You-Doing?'

Ignoring him and his antics, I keep my eyes on the young man trying to maintain as much eye contact as possible. I learned in my class that eye contact oozes truthfulness to the person receiving you. And God knows that I need that right now. If he can see me as truthful and honest, maybe he'll feel at ease to level with me.

Darn-the-luck, I must've been wrong, because before I know it, the flat the barrel of the gun is pointed squarely at me. "I don't think that concerns you," peeps the young man, as slow and as calculated as can be. But that's okay; I know how to play this game.

Winding the cord behind my back, I manage to crack a smile and breathe a sigh before my next comment, "Oh, so we're a tough guy today, huh? So tell me, what's the plan anyway?" I say as I shrug my shoulders while still trying my best to assume control. "To steal from us? Rob us blind?"

"You're walking a thin line. If I were you, I'd—"

"Yeah, but you're not," trying my best to seem as unbothered as ever. Be strong, you got this. I just know it. "You might as well get out while you can. Seriously, what are you going to do? Kill us?"

"You know, if it'll shut your mouth, I just might."

Wow, he really seems serious right now. But according to my training, aggression is good. 'If I anger you, I've got your attention.' And that's all I need right now, his attention. If I can keep his attention long enough, I just might be able to talk him down. While still winding up the cord behind me, I'm still waiting for the right moment to strike.

"Oh, angry are we? Good God call the police!" I say, trying to sound sarcastic and cool. "You know, this really isn't a good look for you. With murder and robbery on your record, you'll probably never see daylight. Which sounds like a waste if you ask me."

"Nobody's asking you."

"Yeah, I know. That's why I said it anyway."

Now getting up from his seat coming straight towards me, I've finally gotten him right where I want him. Just as he tugs my arm, probably trying to drag me some place out of sight, I glance over at Brian who's obviously going to let him do it for fear of his own life. I tell you, what's the need of a man if he can't handle situations like this. But that's okay.

"You're coming with me," he boasts.

And with one fell swoop, I use my free hand to dangle the cord around his neck. Just as it latches on, I pull, but amazingly, he's way stronger than I anticipated. It takes both of his hands to wiggle out of the cord itself, which gives me enough them to dart off for the door. Reaching the door, I swing it open and head straight for the driveway.

Not really knowing what's to come of Brian, I call out for him. "Brian!" Not really willing to stop. While trying to secure my own freedom, I'm not about to risk it all for him; nope, not a chance! Just as I reach the clearing, it happens.

Bang! Bang!

Hitting the floor, I quickly hand search my body, no wounds here! But before I can gather enough energy to run again, I feel a tug of my hair jerking me back to the situation at hand. With the gun now jammed in my right cheek, all movement ceases.

"If you move a muscle, I swear that'll be the last thing you remember. I'm done playing around," he snaps throwing me face down to the ground, to secure my hands this time. With a loop here and a knot there, he's finally finished. Then he pulls me up and throws me into the back seat of the vehicle closest to us which happens to be my Black Sedan. "Come on little lady, we're heading for a ride." Shutting the passenger door, he turns back to me. "Where's the extra set of keys? I know your kind, nice house, multiple cars; you have keys stashed on top of keys. Now where are they?"

Feeling it thoroughly useless to lie, I docile down and tell the truth. "It's up under the arm rest."

Retrieving the keys, he starts the car and down the road we go. Using my car phone, he makes a call. After about two or three rings, the person on the other end finally decides to pick up, "Yeah," says the other person echoing through the car speakers. From the sounds of things, it sounds like the short guy again.

"Hey, Mike, I had to pull out for a few. I'm headed to the bypass, where do you want me to go from there?"

"Just lay low for a minute man. I still have to clean up here."

"Did you find it?"

"Nah, but I'm not leaving here without it though. I'll hit you up on my way out."

"Alright, one."

And with that, the conversation is over. What in the world is 'one' anyway? I mean is that some ghetto translation for the word 'bye' or something? I tell you, these street hoodlums are always trying to re-invent something. And yet with all of their smarts and brains, they still can't seem to make it out to the house of God. Good grief!

Looking through the rearview mirror, he locks eyes with me. "Yo, I'm not familiar with this side of town. So I'm asking you, I know I shouldn't, but I am. Where is the best place to lay low 'round here? And don't play with me."

In a situation like this, only one place comes to mind. So with a deep breath, I reluctantly reply, "1603 Craddleson Way."

Chapter Two

Kid

Sitting in the parking lot of an old playground, my mind has the tendency to run around and around. Man, how did I get myself into this predicament? Was it something that I said? Or was something that I did? All I ever wanted to do was to go through life humble and low-key, but hanging with Mike, my future is crying out with every single plea. How did one errand turn into a nightmare on end? Now, I'm diving deeper and deeper into the biggest mistake of my life. First kidnap and assault, then vandalism, mixed with robbery or so I thought, and finally it's grand theft auto, 'cause I ain't going down for no murder. But with the way that things are going, I'm running out of options quick, fast, and in a hurry.

Looking at my watch, two hours have long since passed, and this woman is the most worrisome person that I've ever known. Every five seconds it's something: I got to pee; I'm hungry; my hands hurt. . .yelp, yelp. One minute she's praying, and the next minute she's fussing. Make up your mind already. I mean, can't she just sit down in peace and let me think. Good God!

"You know, I'd be worried if I were you. No matter how it goes, this situation is bound to end badly. You might as well—"

"Again with the suggestions. I wonder were you as forthcoming when your husband was going around racking up bill after bill with all of them promissory notes."

Looking taken aback, she stares at me blankly.

"Oh what, are we speechless now? Yeah, I said it."

"What bills? What are you talking about?"

"Oh what, you're playing dumb now? Your husband has been going around town for the longest placing this bet and that one. Acting like some Beverly Hills Pimp, making enemies of the streets."

"So that's why we're here. Money? Well that's all you had to say. Good grief just give me a number?"

"What?"

"Give me a number and we can finally be through with this whole charades skit you got going." As agitated as she sounds, it's clear to me that she doesn't quite grasp the reality of the situation yet.

Half laughing to myself, which judging by her looks in the rear view mirror, angers her even more, I manage to speak. "You really don't get it. Do you?"

"Get what?" she yells in her defense.

Turning to face her now, seeing as how we're trapped out here and all, I might as well level with her, "Are you serious right now? Ol' dude has you that fooled. What, you think that I don't have anything else better to do?" Seeing her twisted lip, roll-my-eyes-if-I-wanna type of face, it's clear that she really *doesn't*. But being unbothered, I continue.

"Look, I didn't get out of bed because your husband wrote a few bad checks. This goes way deeper than that." Just as I'm about to throw the trump card, I see it. All of that love and trust that she has in ol' dude. Bad as I want to clear my mind right now, I sure don't want to be the one to break it. So with a deep sigh, I quickly glance away, trying to find something, anything to distract my attention.

"Man, both of ya'll are some looney-tunes for real. Straight out the wood work, I promise you. I mean, who rides a truck this nice, with woodgrain, and leather interior and hangs a wad of pennies on the rearview mirror?" I say pointing at the string of pennies dangling in front of me.

Calming down, she rolls her eyes once again before replying, "Those aren't just pennies. Those there are purple pennies."

Looking at the pennies again making sure that I didn't miss a thing before my next remark, "Purple? Man, these pennies are brown bronzemen's all right."

"Ha! Ha, smart guy. They're made with purple tint, whereas they look like pennies, feel like pennies, but they're worthless in value on the market. The truth is, most people really don't know the difference between that and the real thing. My momma's name was Kenya. She gave it to me as a gift, the day that I preached my first sermon. That's been probably about a year, year and half ago."

"You're a pastor?"

Laughing half-heartedly to herself, she replies, "Yeah, something like that. I'm actually an Evangelist to be politically correct. Anyway, my momma gave them to me. I always thought that it was because she hated Brian so much. According to her, he was never a 'good' match for me. Whatever that means? But she said that she gave it to me so that I would always remember that 'people ain't always what they portray to be.' Anybody can look like the real thing, talk like the real thing, but it's a whole 'nother thing to *be* the real thing."

"Oh I get it, you're on that real McCoy type of junk, huh?"

"I guess so," she answers as she smiles at me for the first time. You know, other than her constant ranting, and relentless complaining, she's all right. Maybe if we'd met on completely different terms, things would be a lot different, but hey, you live and you learn. Good grief, kidnapping a preacher, I'm never going to be able to live that down. Turning back in my seat, I muffle up a few words feeling it to be my time to talk.

"So, where's your mom now? She seems like a real trooper to give you something like that as a present." We both burst out laughing, and for a moment there the reality of things sort of dies down.

"We'll, to be completely honest with you, we weren't that close. But uh, she died a few months back."

"Oh gosh. I'm sorry to hear that."

"Don't be. That's God's will."

"Man, that's harsh. Well, how was the funeral?"

"I wouldn't know. I didn't get to go?"

"Why not?'

"Well, I was up for this big promotion, which I did get by the way, and I just couldn't afford to break away at the moment."

"Not even for your own mother. Man that sucks."

"Well, that's life." Feeling the silence that followed to be somewhat throbbing, she makes the first move to keep the conversation going. "I'm Patricia by the way, Patricia Parker, but most people call me Trish. So, they call you 'Kid', huh?"

Stunned that she knows my name, I swirl around somewhat surprised. "Huh?"

"Your name, Kid?"

"Oh yeah, well . . . " I let my words trail off now second guessing whether or not I should actually reveal my true identity to a person that I kidnapped, but all the more, talking does make the time go by faster. So with a deep sigh, I continue, "My real name is Devon, Devon Harris. And that guy that I was with earlier, yeah he's my uncle. He stepped in when my dad died. He taught me everything I know from bike riding, to playing ball, to—"

". . . robbing people, breaking into their houses, stealing their cars . . . oh yeah, that's totally normal."

Not paying her any attention, I continue, "But uh, I used to watch a whole lot of westerns with my pops as a child. I used to go around playing cowboy everywhere I went, always imitating Billy the Kid. He was a great man. He was like the Scarface for the hood." as I begin to chuckle to myself. You know, I hate to admit it, but those were some good times.

"Anyway, whenever people saw me, they just started calling me 'Billy the Kid.' As I grew though, most people just chopped it up to 'Kid.'"

"Wow, a real cowboy?"

"Yeah, I used to be anyway."

"So you're a cowboy by day and an amateur bad boy at night. Really, I don't get you."

"Get me? Wait hold up a minute, who are you calling amateur?"

"What street dude you know kidnaps a woman, ties her up, and then is fool enough to tell her your real name?"

Straightening up in my seat, whether I want to admit it or not, she's right.

"You know, since we're on a first name basis and all, I really think that we can lose the hand ties, don't you think?" she asks looking at me with the most earnest eyes.

All in all, she seems cool, so against my better judgment, I reach back and untie her anyway. Once free, she climbs into the passenger seat. Seeing my eyes still fixed on her, she turns to me and says, "What? You think that I'm going to let some fool boy drive my brand new truck and I not ride shot gun? Please. . ."

Unsure of what to do next, I turn around. "Aren't you going to take off and run like a wild woman?

"I could, but then again this truck ain't paid off yet," she admits locking eyes with me, and we both burst out laughing. "Besides, I still want to know why we're even in this mess?" she says, looking at me more seriously for an answer.

Clearing my throat, I stick to my first mind, and plead the fifth. "Some things are better left unsaid you know. I just want this whole thing to be over, so that I can get on with my life."

"And what's that? You look sort of young, but not young enough to still be in school. So what do you do?"

"Lots of things you know. It pays to be a Mr. Fix-It where I'm from."

"And where's that?"

"A ways away from here, that's for sure. Brand new cars, two story home, with a Picasso in your house. You've got a Picasso in your house!"

"It didn't always start out like that, believe me. We had to. . .I had to work hard for that."

"How did you do that? You don't look much older than me, and I'm 28."

"Oh well, I got you by a year. God was truly on my side to say the least. But enough about me, what's with you? You just don't look like you fit this lifestyle."

"Well, I didn't chose the life, it choose me," as I turn to her half-smiling.

"But what does that even mean. Everything we do comes by a choice."

"Maybe for some people, but not for everybody."

Ring! Ring! Hearing the car phone ring, I gladly move to answer it, anxious to get off this topic. Some people believe in the power of choice while others like me, you know the ones that live in the real world, just float by the waves trying their best to stay below the radar.

Ring! Ring!

"You should probably answer that."

Pressing the talk button, I answer "Yo, what's good?"

"Excuse me. Hello, Brian? Trish is that you?"

Looking wide eyed from one to another, both of us are clueless as to what we should do next. She opts to take the reins on this one. "Hey, Pastor Thomas is that you?"

"Yeah, how are you? We missed you tonight?"

Looking at me, she continues. Man this is bad, real bad. If she ever wanted to out me, this would be the perfect time to do so. But amazingly, she doesn't.

"Well uh, you know Pastor something kind of serious came up. You know that it had to be serious for me to miss."

"Yeah, yeah I know. Well, I'm praying that all is well with you and your family. Give Deacon Brian my regards, and uh, I'll see you later. But 'ay Evangelist, is the offer still a possibility for you."

"Oh yes, Pastor, now you know that I haven't changed my mind about that."

"Ok well, take care of things over the next few days and I'll see you on Monday."

"Alright, take care Pastor."

"You too. Have a good night." And with that, the call is over.

Looking at her questionably, I have to ask, "So, you had a situation? I thought you were smart Evangelist. That was your time to spill the beans."

"I would've, but against all odds, I refuse to believe that this is you. And if that is the case, I at least want to give you the opportunity to reach your potential. And besides, forgiveness is for everybody."

Before I can even respond, the phone rings again.

Ring! Ring!

Feeling this to again be my duty, I take the call. "Hello," I answer trying to answer the phone a little more civilized this time.

"Yo man, what's up?" Feeling somewhat dissatisfied to be speaking with only Mike, I dial back into my regular tone of voice.

"Yeah man, you alright? You've been out of the network for about three or so hours now, what's the hold up?"

"Man this fool trying to play me like some street hub or something. He don't know this and he don't know that."

"Shoot, he better know something." Careful not to get into too much detail in front of Trish. "Well man, what are you going to do?"

"What am I going to do? You mean what are we going to do. Man this ain't just my problem. Talk to the wife, see what she knows." Looking at Trish, it's clear that she doesn't know too much, so I proceed.

"I already did; man she's clueless."

"All right man, lets up the stakes. Let's take him by his girl's house over on 612 Milwaukee Lane and—" Trying my best to intercept the call, I pick up the receiver in order to take Mike off of the speakers.

"Yeah. . .yeah. . .sounds good to me. . .yeah sure." For the next minute or two, I try my best to make my responses fairly vague since my replies are now the only ones being heard. Hanging up the phone, it's clear that nothing has escaped Trish. She's sitting up waiting for me like the black ship without a sail.

"His girl? What girl, 'Kid?' I'm his wife, so what girl?"

Not really knowing how to answer, I don't. "Listen, I don't really know if he meant girl, like a girl or like a girl-girl. I'm just uh. . .Well, really what I think he was trying to say—"

"I heard what he said, Kid. Now, I'm asking you, what girl?"

Not wanting to lie to her, I just look down and shake my head. After a few seconds, I guess her private thoughts begin to answer her own questions, because before I know it, paths of tears trail down her cheeks. Not really knowing what to say or do, I don't do anything.

"Well..." she says putting on her seat belt, "...you heard the man, 612 Milwaukee Lane."

I'm half stunned and half scared. Not really knowing what this woman is capable of, I ask for confirmation, "Come again?"

"Did I stutter?" she asks snapping her fingers and rolling her neck like she's Mrs. Diva-on-wheels. One look in her eyes, you can see the anger building up on the inside, but feeling her to be a woman scorned, it's only right that she knows the truth. And what better way than to show her for herself?

"Yes, ma'am. Milwaukee Lane it is." Cranking up, we drive off into the night. This time, on a different mission; not one of power and money, but on a path to discover the truth. Well, if truth be told, I already know the truth, but it's high time that she gets to see her husband for what he really is for herself.

Driving off into the distance, my eyes lock in on the purple pennies hanging from the rearview mirror. Whether she knew it or not, her momma knew more than what she let on.

Sway pennies sway. . .Sway pennies sway. . .

Chapter Three

Trish

Pulling up to the house, I can't help but feel that I've been here before. With the green shutters, oval glass window, and middle-class housing, I know this place. I just can't place it right now. As we slow to a stop, my mind is rambling as I struggle to come up with what question to ask first. It's crazy, my mind knows, but my heart just isn't ready to accept the fact that my husband, the man that I've hand carried these last three years, has found someone else. With tears rolling from my eyes, I try my best to think of something, anything that could have led to this. I've been riding with him for three years, sleeping in the same bed with him every night, waking up every morning and having him put his feet under my breakfast table. At what point did he decide that this wasn't working for him? At what point did he decide that I wasn't enough for him? At what point did he decide. . .that he wasn't. . .happy? At what point?

"Aye, you all right?" Kid asks interrupting my thoughts.,

I quickly wipe off my flushed face and pull myself together. "Yeah, yeah, I'm fine."

"You sure?"

Feeling irritated now, I turn to him in a ball of anger. "Yeah, I said I was. I'm good, really. . .I am."

In the midst of my feelings, Kid leans over and grabs my hand. Almost instantly my wall of pain falls down, and the tears begin to flow yet again. Obviously knowing nothing else to do, he squeezes my hand a little tighter for a little longer. And in all honesty, I can't believe this. I'm being emotional counseled by some two-bit thug probably barely making enough money to pay his own rent. But, desperately needing someone at the moment, he'll have to do, and to tell you the truth, I don't mind. After suffering to watch me wail like some lost and found pig, he finally straightens up to talk. "Hey, I'm going to go in here for a minute and talk to her. I'll be back in a few."

Stopping him dead in his tracks, I say, "What do you mean, you'll be back in a few? I'm coming with you."

"I don't really feel like this is the best time—"

"Who cares about what you feel? That's my husband, so yes, I'm going with you." Fluffing my hair in the mirror one last time, I fix my clothes and jump out of the truck, "Come on. Let's go."

Seeing that his oppositions are going nowhere, he finally gets out and follows me to the door. Once we reach the door however, he steps in front of me. "You probably should let me do most of the talking."

Feeling that to be more of a command rather than a suggestion, I quickly take my place and follow his lead. And taking my current state of mind into consideration, who knows what's going to come out of my mouth. Feeling his eyes still on me, I utter up some type of response. "Yeah, yeah, that's fine," I reply trying to sound as convincingly calm as I can.

"And one more thing."

"What?" highly frustrated at this point.

"You probably should wear my hoodie," he replies taking off his hoodie and handing it to me.

Puzzled, I ask, "Why?"

"Well, let's just say it's not so inviting to see someone come up to your door at 2 in the morning with bloody clothes."

Looking down at my dress, I have to agree with him. So without question, as he rings the doorbell, I put on the hoodie, which smells strongly of Axe body spray. Gee weeze, you'd think that these guys would know when to lay off. I mean good God, enough is enough.

Ding- Dong, Ding-Dong. . .no answer.

Ding-Dong, Ding-Dong. . .still no answer.

Ding-Dong, Ding-Dong. . .feeling this to be somewhat pointless, I pull him back, "Aye Kid, come on. Whoever's in there has obviously went to bed already. Let's just go and come—"

Just before I can get the words out of my mouth, the door cracks open, and a woman with a night robe answers the door. Even in the dim light, I can make out her features. Kid goes on rambling about something or another, but I just can't get past this. Out of all of the women in the church, he chose her. Out of all of the women in the street, he chose her. Looking wide-eyed, her eyes lock with mine, which I don't know how good that is at the moment, because my mouth is still fly-wide opened. Recognizing my face, she steps up to hug me, but all I can do is cry. Out of everyone, he chose her. . .Danielle Thomas, the Pastor's daughter. The same woman that I ministered to. The same woman that I spoke words of comfort to when that no good dog left her in the streets barefoot and pregnant. The same woman that I would give my last for. The same woman that would eat under my table. The same woman that I stuck my neck out for just to help her get a decent job. Really, Brian? Really?

Releasing me, she stands back smiling, but after looking me in the face, she knows that something's off. Kid tries his best to cover and offers up his brand of rubbish, but for the first time in a while, I'm speechless.

Staring at me, she says, "Evangelist Parker, are you ok?" as she attempts to rub my shoulder in comfort with a soft gentle sway. God Lord, now I know what Jesus must've felt when He looked at Judas. Oh good Lord, help me. Feeling myself to be in way too deep to lie, I just spit out. "Are you sleeping with my husband?"

Taking off of her feet obviously, she drops both her hands and her smile as she tries her best to conjure up some kind of hog wash. "Uh, well. . .Trish, you know that I would—"

Not really in the mood for any type of excuses, I repeat myself. "Are you sleeping with my husband?"

Standing there like a deer in head lights, she answers, "It was just a mistake. . .You know me, Trish. I would never do anything to hurt you. . .You know that. . .It just—"

Half laughing to myself, I get lost in my thoughts yet again. Standing here crying and what not, I'm the one who's been in the blind. Chic, what are you crying for. The nerve of some people I tell you. Keep calm, Trish. Keep calm. Cutting her off in the middle of her spill, it just comes out. "How long?"

"Trish believe me—"

"How long?" I repeated yelling at this point. Calm Trish has left the building.

"A little over two years."

Feeling my legs get weak from under me, I lean on the bench sitting in front of the door. Kid rushes to my side.

"Are you alright?"

Looking up at him, I just shake my head.

"It started out as just a simple mistake, one thing just led to another. I've tried to stop, honest I did. . .but it's not that easy," she says coming closer to me.

"How do you try not to sleep with someone else's husband?"

"It's just so complicated right now—"

"Complicated?"

"Trish. . . . we have a son."

"A son? You don't have but one child and—" stopping myself in my own tracks, I realize right then and there that the baby that I've been seeing for the past year, playing with for the past year, babysitting when she had to work for the past year, has been my husband's son. Out of all of the things that he could have done, he had a baby. I wanted a baby. . .I wanted HIS baby. I'm the one who went through two miscarriages. I'm the one who went from doctor to doctor trying to make this thing possible. I'm the one that went to the adoption agencies, and all the while, I've had to listen to him rage and rant about how he doesn't want any children. I'm confused. Did he not want a child because he already had one or did he just not want a child with me?

Listening to this cut me deeper than a knife itself. Sitting down now, my breath leaves me making it harder to breathe. . .harder to see. And if that's not enough, she continues. Don't she know that we ain't Catholic? There's no need to confess it all. "I tried to get. . .believe me. . ." She continues now kneeling before me. "I never wanted this to come in between our friendship, honest. . .I've went to the mothers for prayer, even to my father about this—"

"Woo, woo, wait a minute...you mean to tell me that everyone knows but me." Now standing, it's amazing how one spare moment of anger can spur on several ounces of strength. "It' s not enough to play me like a fool, but you make a mockery of me in my own place of worship. . .embarrass me in front of the people that I know and love! Oh No!"

Turning to Kid, I say, "You know what, you're going to have to take it from here. Because if I don't leave now, God knows what I'm going to do." Not even waiting for him to reply, I turn and head towards the truck.

Still not relenting, she comes behind me anyway. "Trish wait—" and it happens, before she can even get two words out of her mouth, my fist meet her right in the gaper. As she falls to the ground, my anger's too far gone to stop now so the fighting continues. Out of the blue, I feel someone pulling me up, it's Kid of course, but still screaming and kicking, this is no time to quit.

"Stop it you two!" he yells coming in between us now. "Both of you, get a grip." Now gaining both of our attention, he turns first to Danielle. "Don't you know that God does things decent and in order? God's not going to give you something that's already taken. Now I haven't been to church in a while myself, but I know enough to know that what GOES around. . . COMES around. He messed over a good wife to get to you. What makes you think that he won't do that to you?"

"You don't know him. He loves me. We have a son together; we have a son!"

"Oh, Boo-Hoo. Don't nobody care about that but YOU! You know, women like you kill me. You'll settle for a piece of a man instead of waiting patiently for someone who's willing to give you the whole thing."

Now turning to me, he continues. "And you, I thought that you knew better than this. Fighting, yelling, and fussing. . .all this over a man?"

"You don't understand, he's my husband. He was my everything. How could—"

"Oh, I understand. But, you're a woman of God and a true one as far as I can see. Rule 101 of relationships, 'you never let a man take you that low.' Talking about he's your husband, he's your everything… God is your everything. And by now you should know that if someone is willingly going to walk out of your life, YOU LET THEM!!! Stop keeping people that don't want to be kept. Now if truth be told, God sent you signs along the way."

Looking at him, I'm way too far gone to process much of anything.

"God always sends signs before destruction. Just thank Him that He revealed all this to you when He did. 'Cause honestly, it could be a lot worse. I don't know how much worse it can get, but it can get there."

Looking at him, I can't help but smile. But strangely, he's right.

Now repositioning himself, he gets back to his lecture, this time turning back to Danielle. "Now, I really came out here to ask you this. It's very, very important that you answer me truthfully. I know that you've been several places with Brian, and spent an awful amount of time with him. Did you, by any chance, see him with a black box or hear him mention anything about Pack N' Play, code presses, or anything of that nature?"

"No, no I haven't. Why? What's wrong? Is he in some kind of trouble of something?"

"Ma'am, that's what we're trying to keep him out of. Are you sure that you don't know anything? Anything at all?"

"No, no. . . I don't."

"Well, I guess that's it then," Kid says moving toward the vehicle. "You have a nice night ma'am." And with that, we leave.

No, I'm leaving all of my problems, my marriage, and my frustration. I'm leaving it all right there on this very spot. I really don't know what's going to become of Brian or even what he's gotten himself into but one thing's for sure, I no longer care. Not about him, not about anything. It's like everything that I've believed in, everything that I'd worked so hard for, it's all a lie. A purple tinted hope of a future that is never really going to come. I guess that in the end, the only one that believed that it would was me.

Looking at the purple pennies as they jingle from side to side on the rearview mirror, I can't help but think of how my mother was right. Dog-gone-it she was actually right! She was literally the only person around me to call out my life for what it truly is. . .a purple tinted lie. And just to think of it, she knew it all along. She knew. While others smiled in my face and probably laughed at me behind my back, saying, 'Hey, there she is, Trish, the fool.' She knew. . .she really knew.

Chapter Four

Kid

Driving back isn't as fun as it was driving up to say the least. It's that dark, lonely, and distant kind of peace; to the point where no one is talking, not even me. But oddly, we both seem to be feeling the weight of the situation that has come to be. I, for one, feel my freedom falling fast between the spaces of time. While Trish, on the other hand, feels her life fading by and by. Everything that she knew and everything that she'd hoped for all seems to crumbling at the sound of destiny's voice. I wish that I could help her, but at this point, I can't even help myself. It's crazy how life can change with just one simple choice.

"Hey, I just talked with Mike. We're headed to meet him and Brian at 'Pack N' Play' on Parker's Way." Looking over to the passenger seat, it's like she doesn't even hear me. She's still turned facing the window, motionless from what I can see. Feeling the distance between us, I guess it's up to me to continue the conversation, so I do. "But hey, we've been riding around for hours and I'm kind of tired. So uh, do you want to stop by the store and get some coffee or something? Maybe even something to eat?" I ask glancing back over to her, but still nothing. "Is that a yes? Maybe even a No?"

"Nah, I'm good." Finally feeling content enough to speak.

Ring! Ring! Checking the phone yet again.

Ring! Ring!

"Hello." Hearing no answer, I feel compelled to repeat myself. "Hello?"

"Hey, young fellow. I believe that I spoke with you earlier. This is Pastor Thomas, is Evangelist Parker available by any chance?"

"Hold on for a minute." Muting the receiver, I turn her way, and by the way that she's shaking her head, I can tell that it's a no. So obediently, I unmute the phone and relay the message. "No sir, she's not. Can I take a message?"

"No that's alright. I'll just try again later."

"Ok, sounds good." Clicking off, I straighten back up in my seat.

"Well, it's clear that she's relayed the message to daddy." Glancing over to Trish, who by the looks of things finds it to be somewhat amusing.

"Yep, I guess she did."

"Well, here we are," I say as we pull up to the spot.

"What is this?"

"Pack N' Play."

"Oh yeah, I can see that." she quips nudging me in irritation. "I mean, what is this place? I mean look at it, it's not exactly welcoming."

Looking up at the place, I had to agree with her. With the dull paint colors, and nearly empty parking lot, one would think that it's on the verge of being condemned.

"Ah sucks, that's just the daylight hitting it. You should see this place at night. Man, this place be booming. This is where all the serious card players, gambling, and dealers hang out at. This place be sitting on crazy cash man."

"Mmm, you would think with all that someone would find the time to do some home improvements."

"Ha! Ha! Yeah, I guess you're right," I counter easing off my seatbelt. Looking over the parking lot, we're the only car, so it's clear that Mike hadn't gotten here yet. To tell you the truth though, I'm actually kind of glad about it. At least now, we can actually just you know, talk. "So..." I glance at Trish, my way of preparing her for a lengthy convo. "It's officially Saturday."

"Yeah, so?"

"What do you mean so? It's 7am on a Saturday morning. I mean, what would you be doing right about now?"

"Me? Ha, sleep!" she answers and giggles.

"What about you? Would you be sleeping the day away?"

"Who me? Nah, I'm an early bird really."

"No!"

"Yeah, for real though. Plus I live with my momma, and she be stomping around the house at about 5:30am. So, you know there's no sleep going on there."

"Wait a minute! Wait...so you mean to tell me that you live with your momma."

"Yep."

"Wow, seriously? That's embarrassing."

"Well, I wasn't always at home. Things just sort of happened that way I guess."

"Well...do tell."

"Ok, ok. So, I finished school—"

"Oh, a college man."

"Ah no, not me. I knew college wasn't for me a long, long time ago."

"Why not?"

"Aren't you the one for questions today?"

"Well, what can I say? You did kidnap me against my will, sooooo the least you can do is answer a few questions," I say shrugging my shoulders in a playful sort of way.

"Yeah, yeah, you got me. Well, my dad passed in my junior year, and my mom wasn't fit to work no how. I mean, she did a few odd jobs, but I don't think that she stayed sober enough to hold a permanent gig. Anyway, once I graduated, I went straight to work. From dish washer, to mechanic, to plumbing, I mean anything that paid. A couple years into that however, I met someone. We got married and all but it wasn't too long before that crashed and burned."

"What happened?"

"She left." He pauses taking a minute to let the words to take effect. I haven't thought about that in a while. And to tell you the truth, I never knew how much that still hurt until the words just rolled out of my mouth.

"Oh, I'm sorry to hear that."

"Oh don't be. She said that she couldn't see herself married to a dreamer. I guess she was right in a way. I mean, I was so focused on my maybe's that I really couldn't manage a stable environment long enough for us to have anything."

"That's tough."

"No, not really. It may sound crazy to you, but now that we aren't together, I finally have my stuff together."

"Really? Kidnapping and breaking and entering is having your stuff together?"

"Ha! Ha! I see you got jokes." And we both burst into laughter. "Nah, but this ain't really me. This is just some big-big mistake that just went too far. I mean, don't get me wrong. I do divulge in my share of mischief, but nothing this extreme. You know, I just shoot a couple games of craps here, mixed with some poker and spades, and maybe even a little casino crashing, but I never dab in more than my pockets can handle. Now your husband, he's off the charts. He be coming in places like he's Tarzan or something throwing all kind of money on the table. And after meeting ya'll, I really just don't see why. I mean, does he pay or fix anything?"

"Do you want the truth?"

"Wow, well I guess that's a no."

Honk! Honk! Looking across the lot, in pulls Mike in a red four door. Looks like we're back to reality. Glancing over to Trish, it's clear that she knows what's coming. The scared-worried look now covers her face. It's like the very sight of Mike just confirmed her fate. It's like we never left the house, in which she ran in fear. It's like nothing changed, she's the victim and I'm the man with the gun threatening her every move. But God knows that I can't do that. She's a minister for crying out loud. Her blood's not going to be on me. Leaning over to her, I say, "Hey, you ready?"

Looking wide-eyed at me, sort of surprised, she manages to speak. "Aren't you going to tie me up or something? Drag me in chained and bound?"

Laughing more to myself than anything, I turn back to her and smile. "If you don't get out this car, I just might. Ha-ha!" Feeling relieved, she begins to laugh too.

As we near the walk way, out comes Mike with Brian. All bloody nosed and bound, ole' dude still hasn't cracked, but all that's about to change. As I watch Trish walk a little ways in front of me, obviously taking notice of her husband's appearance, I stagger just a few steps back. Think fast Kid! Think fast.

"Yo Kid, you good? You ready or what?" yells Mike, clearly trying to see who's side I'm on.

"No worries man, I got this!" I reply as I slowly remove the revolver from my right side, cuffing it in dead silence. "Yeah, I got it." And with one swift move, I get into position. "I got it." At that very moment, Trish turns back, but it's too late.

Wap!

"Trish!" yells Brian trying his best to save his wife, but again he's just a second too late.

With the butt of the gun, like a baseball bat hitting a homerun, my swing comes full circle. And with that one hit, Trish falls to the floor, lying lifeless. She never knew what hit her; she never even had the chance.

"Ha! Ha! Man, you had me worried there for a minute? I thought that you were getting some clear conscience on me or something."

"Nah, never that." And we both burst out laughing.

Brian, helpless enough, breaks down in complete shock. For the first time through this whole ordeal, it's finally clear to him the kind of situation that he's in. And finally, we see the fearful respect that we deserve…now we're getting somewhere.

As Mike pulls Brian, who now refuses to walk into the casino, I'm left standing outside. Seeing Trish on the ground in front of me shook me there for a minute. Poor sister, she didn't deserve any of this but she just had to be married to that dope.

"Man, God!" Now feeling the pressure of having to think on my feet, I bend down beside her. From a distance, she doesn't even appear to be breathing, but as I lift her up, she is. Glancing up from time to time to make sure that nobody's watching me, I take a Kleenex from my pocket and wipe her face before lifting her onto my shoulder. "Hang in there baby girl. It'll be over before you know it." Think fast Kid! Think fast.

Chapter Five

Trish

"Trish! Trish!" cries the voice, though barely noticeable to me at the moment, because the pain's too bad. Good Lord, okay one move at a time. "Trish! Trish!" from where I am it's hard to tell whether that's a murmur or a whisper. Speaking of where I am, where am I? No lights, just blank. But it smells awful, Jesus Christ. "Trish! Trish! Baby, are you ok?"

Squinting my eyes, I'm not sure. "Yeah, yeah…I guess so."

"Trish! Trish!"

"Brian?"

"Trish! Trish! That's you, ah thank—" Nah, who else is it? The Easter Bunny? "Look baby, I'm going to get us out of here, just give—"

"Brian, where am I? What's going on?" I ask pushing the wall above me. Call me crazy but it feels like I have walls all around me. "What? Oh my God, am I in a box?"

"Look baby, I know that it looks bad right now, but—"

"Looks bad? I'm in a box!" I yell, officially frantic.

"Yeah, baby I know. But listen, just keep your voice down okay. They might hear you and—"

"Keep my voice down. I'm not going to keep my voice down!" I say even though I'm out of options and unsure of what to do next. I'm tired of running scared; it's get-out-girl mode. I may not be able to see, but I can still move. Feeling the texture around me, it feels to be every bit of wood. Wood, I can get out of that. Time to go to work! And with every bit of strength in me, I start kicking the crate, hitting the wooden frame, and yelling and screaming to the top of my lungs trying to get somebody, anybody's attention. "Hey!" I scream in between pats.

"Trish! Trish! Baby please—"

"Hey! Let me OUT of HERE!" I continue to scream in between pats.

"Trish come on, please!"

"Hey! Hey! Let me out!"

"Trish! Trish! Stop"

Now turning my attention to Brian who's just annoying as ever, I yell, "Oh, for heaven's sake, hush! You're not the one stuck in here. So, please spare me!"

"Trish! Trish! Please don't—"

But even as he speaks, the lock on the door turns and the door opens. Unable to move, we both sit still, dead silent.

Pat! Pat! Judging from the weight of the pats, it's hard to tell exactly which one it is.

Pat! Pat! Hearing the pats, I'm unsure as to who the person is actually coming to see: him or me? Tightening my fists, I'm not running scared anymore. If he opens this box, I'm coming out with everything I've got.

But listening out, the pats stop. Oh good, it's Brian's turn now. He'll be alright.

"Look here, I'm tired of playing around with you, ok…"

"Oh, that's Kid. What does he want?"

"So, I'm going to give you one time, and one time only…" as he flicks what sounds like a lighter. Probably taking a minute to light him a cigarette, I guess. "The cold presses…Where they at?" he asks as he takes a minute to let the silence take effect. Like he's some macho-man or something, boy please!

"Look, I told ya'll ok…I don't know nothing about no—" cries Brian. Hearing him plead for what might very well be the last few moments of his life, poor guy, I almost pity him.

"Come on! Come on, man. It's me, okay. I know you have them."

"I don't know nothing about no cold presses—"

"Ahhh, sure you do. They're some nice packages, about yea high. . . .with a nice range of cocaine and smack inside of 'em, bitter-raw before it even hits the market. You know the ones that your girl drained dry." Judging from his tone, I'm guessing that he's talking about Danielle right now. Man, who knew that the pastor's daughter is a sherm head? Oh Lord, this just gets better and better. "Oh, there's no need to look to Trish. She already knows. We took a short little trip over there this afternoon to see her and your son."

Feeling that he's bit off a little bit more than he could chew, Brian turns towards me in the box, "Baby, she meant nothing to me. I promise you baby! Don't—"

"I'm pretty sure that she's clear on things, player. Your girl wasted no time filling her in. Now, where are the cold presses?"

"Man, I told you. I don't know—"

"Okay, ok. . . ." he says now getting a little agitated himself, obviously. "Ok, that's fine with me."

"What are you doing? No! What are you doing?" hearing Brian plea, I'm not really sure what's going on. Well, that's until I feel the box move. He's taking me. "No! No! I'll give you anything. What is it? Money, cars, man anything but my wife! Please."

Still pulling me, Kid manages to reply. "I don't want anything. I want the COLDPRESSES!"

"Man please, I promise—" Brian's pleas kept getting fainter and fainter by the second. Wherever we were headed, it can't be good. And then suddenly, we stop.

As I sit motionless for the next few minutes, it's not entirely clear to me what's going on yet. But still I wait, for what I know is coming.

Bang! Bang!

Jesus Christ, who is that beating on the crate? I cradle myself in the space and shield my eyes from the blows that barely miss me.

Bang! Bang!

"Oh God!" I scream shrieking to the top of my lungs as the last swing of a hammer cracks the crate wide open. Nothing is left but my frail body that was inside. Peaking from beyond my knees, I see Mike and Kid who's still holding the hammer. Just the three of us, yet again.

With a smirk wider than a pack of Cooles, Mike rushes toward me and drags me to a chair. Once he's confident that I'm in place, he straightens and turns to Kid. "Hem her up," he orders giving him the green light to tie me up head to toe.

Without question, Kid drops the hammer and picks up the rope. With Mike standing guard, Kid proceeds to tie me up, from my arms on down.

Not really knowing what else to do, I just look at him. Good grief, I thought that he was more than this. Stepping back into my ministerial shoes, I slip back into my training. If I can't reason with him, I know God can. First things first, call out the situation at hand. . . .got it!

"My, my what do we have here? A sure fire tough guy, huh? Could've fooled me."

Looking up at me, he smirks with a sly devil grin and continues with his work. Glancing around the room, there's nothing. Now how am I supposed to 'flip the tables of control' in this sink hole? But, if it's good enough for Jesus, it's good enough for me. "You know, you can skip the rope and just move on with it, really. I mean, these Boy Scout knots are pretty childish don't you think?"

Glancing up at me again, he's no longer smiling, just staring. Blank aggression, I like it. Any response is a good response, so I've got to keep this up. "You know Devon,--"

Stopping me mid-sentence, Mike steps up, in a flustered mess. "She knows your name?"

Turning back to his uncle in an Oops-I-got-caught sort of way, Kid opens his mouth to explain. But, I think I got this one.

"Oh yeah, I know yours too. One thing I don't get though, where you this dense after your brother's death, or does it just come naturally?"

Looking at me with one hand raised, it's clear that this Mike character has had all that he can take. But just as he gets within 2-3 feet of me, Kid stands up between of us trying his best to shield me. It happened so fast, I don't even think that *he* knows what he just did. I've got him right where I want him.

Turning to his uncle, Kid tries his best to re-vamp the situation, "Take five, and let me handle the rest of this."

"Let you handle this? We're in this because of you! You told her our names and God only knows what else!" yelps Mike as if that justifies his reactions toward me.

"I know, I know. I messed up, okay. But let me finish here and I promise you that she's not going to be doing all this." Looking from Kid to me, it's clear that Mike doesn't trust the suggestion but he goes along with it anyway.

"Five minutes, Kid. Five minutes, he repeats" as he walks toward the door.

"Five it is. I mean, it ain't even going to take three." Waiting until he's sure that his uncle is completely out of sight, Kid turns to me in somewhat of a whisper. "Are you trying to get both of us killed?"

"Both? Then why am I the only one being tied up? Huh?"

He glances back toward the doorway before continuing. "Man, I'm trying to help you and this is how you repay me?"

"Help me? What kind of help is this?"

"Just trust me for a second, alright?"

"Trust you?"

"Yeah, trust me."

"I don't think so! The last time I trusted you, I ended up in a box."

"I had to do that. I couldn't just let you walk in. Mike's my uncle and all but when it comes to what's his, he'll kill me dead—"

"You know, I really expected more from you," I bark cutting him off in mid-sentence. "Don't you see? God's giving you a second chance to relive your life, the right way…His way. Mike's already chosen his path in life, when are you going to choose yours?" It takes a second or two to really get his attention. "What, you think that it's a mistake that we met tonight? No, no way…You were here tonight because you couldn't possibly be anywhere else. God sees you, and—"

"Really? You're going to do this now. We're in the—" trying his best to prove his point.

"I see you, Kid." For a moment, we just stare at one another. But that doesn't last long, because within a few seconds, in comes Mike pulling Brian behind him.

"Hey Kid, we got problems!" Throwing Brian to the floor and locking the door behind him, Mike paces the floor as erratically as ever.

"Yo man, what's up?"

"5-O man!" he cries out pulling the black wall paper from the blinds. "Man look, look outside. It's like four maybe five squad cars out there."

Looking just as lost as a kid on his first day of school, Kid freezes up.

"Kid. . ."

Hearing my voice, he turns back to me. "There's still time. Make a move. "

Thoroughly fed up with me, Mike hurls around in anger, "Ahhh, please shut-up and –"

"Kid. . . All things work for the good of those who love the Lord. All things…"

"Ah man, shut her up or I'll do it for you!" Mike says to Kid, but this time Kid doesn't move. He doesn't move at all.

"Kid, listen to me. Choose this day whom you will serve. Come on Kid, you can't be a screw up all of your life—"

In the middle of me talking, Mike takes his 9mm and heads straight for me. But before he could even get two steps in, Kid pushes him back toward the wall.

"Dude? Seriously, she got you bugging—"

"Kid, there's still time."

Bang! Bang! Hearing the knocks at the door, it's clear that this is not some ordinary call. The police had a good idea of what was taking place and from the sounds of things, they came ready and prepared.

Bang! Bang! With each and every knock, it seems like it just drains the life out of Kid. Poor guy, he'd probably never see daylight and to think that this was all just some big mistake.

"Kid. . ."

He turns to me with his eyes begging for help that in his heart he had little hope for. "Kid, you can still make it out," I say as I lift my hands from behind my back. "Quick, untie me."

"Ahhh man, don't listen to her—"

"Kid, untie me. You don't have much time left." Thoroughly out of options, he does so. Once my hands and feet are free, I immediately begin to fix my hair and face. "Okay, untie Brian and give me your hoodie."

"What? Why?"

"What do you think? That I should just go to the door in a torn and blood-stained dress? Boy please, give me your hoodie."

Not knowing anything else to do, he does. Then he turns to Mike. "Get up, put some of this stuff away and put that gun away."

And with that, I walk toward the door, trying my best to hold everything together. Think Trish, think. With me being just a few feet short of the door, the door swings open and in storms three officers.

"Hands up!"

Not wanting to become a target, I quickly comply. With guns aimed solely for me, they proceed. "You have the right to…Evangelist? Evangelist Parker?"

I open my eyes clearly to see exactly who is calling my name like they know me. Oh Lord, it's Deacon Hamilton. I forgot that he was on the force. "Oh Deac! Lord Jesus, don't scare me like that no more. Ha! Ha!" With both of us laughing, he puts his weapon down.

"Good Lord woman, what in God's name are you doing in these parts? Better yet, what are you doing here at Pac N' Play?"

Not really knowing how to respond, I just flash a quick grin until I can get my thoughts straight.

"I mean, look at you. Your face is all scratched and swollen," he says as he touches my face. "What have you been doing? Fighting? Don't take this the wrong way, but this ain't the look of no saint."

"Huh, don't I know it. Well uh, the truth is, I was uh---"

Before I can even get the words out of my mouth good, out comes the other two officers with Mike and Kid following behind in handcuffs. Brian's walking behind them like he's some great Samaritan or something. God only knows what he told them folks. One thing's for sure, I have to do something fast. As they near me, Kid locks his eyes with mine like I betrayed him or something, so I know that I have to straighten this out. "Whoo, Whoo what are you doing? Where are you taking them?"

The stout police officer looks over to me and he says matter-of-factly, "Oh ma'am, there's no need to worry. You're husband told us everything, we'll take—"

"No, he didn't!" I yell as I pull the officer from the two men. All eyes are officially on me now, Brian's in particular.

"Evangelist you, okay?" asks Deacon Hamilton.

"Oh, she's fine. She just hit her head or something..." exclaims Brian which is crazy to me, because he's been playing hush mouth all night.

"Oh no, I'm good."

"Well ma'am, you're husband explained to us how these two men terrorized the two of you all night and—"

With Kid still looking at me, I had a choice to make.

"Oh, did they?"

"Are you denying this, ma'am?" questions the stout officer.

"I am," I say as boldly as I know how. Lie or not, I knew that I was doing the right thing.

"You are?. . . .Ok, look officer—"

"Ahhh, shut up, Brian." The more I speak, the angrier I become. How dare he?

"Shut-up? . . ."

"Look, is this some kind of game or something? We're just here because we got a call—"

"Game? Officer, no!" Brian says fixing his eyes on Deacon Hamilton now. "Come on, Paul. Look, I don't know why she's lying but if you don't believe me just look at her dress underneath the hoodie. I mean, it's plastered in blood, not to mention that it's a torn hot mess."

"Oh really?" Darn the luck, he had to go there.

"Officer, just look."

"What you mean just look? Boy this is my—"

"Ma'am, please remove the hoodie."

Not really willing to show the rags beneath my clothes, I do nothing at all. No, no Brian. Not this time. Taking my stance, I proudly fold my arms across my chest, a clear sign that I wasn't hearing that crap.

"Ok ma'am, are you resisting an official order—"

"Evangelist…Trish, just take off the hoodie."

Hearing it from Deacon Hamilton, I finally give in. "Fine! Fine, okay," I say taking the hoodie off and the torn scraps that hang across me are now on display for everyone to see.

"See, see, officer I told you—"

"Oh my God! Trish what happened to you?" asks Deacon Hamilton. Seeing the concern in his eyes, I have to level with him. I'm not going to hide behind any purple pennies, no not this time.

"What am I doing here? I'll tell you what I'm doing here. . ." I begin as I look from Brian to Kid, both eyeing me with expectation; each one not really knowing what's about to come out of my mouth. Clearing my throat, I begin to let the words flow, letting the chips fall where they may. "The truth is that on last night, I was waiting for Brian to come home so we could make it to the conference. I got all dressed up because Pastor Thomas was going to announce my big promotion in front of the whole congregation." I look at Brian, who's now clearly thrown for a loop. Maybe that's because he never really believed in me. Turning to him, I continue, "Yeah that's right I got the job." Turning back to the others, I say a silent prayer. "God help me." Then I continue aloud. "And as usual, he was late. So here I am storming around the house, and in he walks with these two." I gesture to the two in handcuffs. "This wide-eyed fool Mike, whose currently rolling his eyes like I'm not talking about him, and this guy, Kid."

Kid just puts his head down like he's accepted the fate that he knows is coming.

"Kid is one of my closest friends."

Kid looks up from the ground like he's just received his last lifeline.

Brian pops out of his cool mode and stands just as blank as a deer in headlights.

Walking over to Kid, I continue. "My friend, who helped me to see past it all." Walking back into my own space, looking squarely at Deac, I feel compelled to tell it. Tell it for the first time, with no tint and no shame. "I don't know how to say this, so I'll just come out with it. My husband's cheating on me." I blurt out now looking dead at Brian, whose eyes beg of me 'not-now' but it's too late for that. "He's been cheating on me, with Danielle, for years."

Watching as Deac puts his head down, it's clear that even he knows. "Oh wow, so you know to?" I quiz him with tears streaming down my face.

"Trish look, I heard about it, but I didn't—"

"Nah, there's no need to explain. There's no need to lie. I'm just done with it. I'm done. You know that he has a baby with her. Yeah, he does. And you know what? I could've dealt with the laziness, the cheating, but what I cannot deal with is lying. He lied to me, stole my money to support his…his baby and that two-timing little—"

"Trish, I know how you must feel right now, but--"

"No, it's ok. I'm fine! I'm good. I'm fine. I've spent all night, trying to fight for my marriage, trying to find something worth holding onto…but I've got nothing. My husband is a liar, a cheater, and a drug addict." Stopping now, it's funny, 'cause even I'm shocked on how that just rolled off of my tongue, but hey, I'm in too deep to stop now. "I'm here today, in this crappy building right now with all of them trying my very best to get my husband to kick his habit."

"What? That's insane. Officers, I really don't know—"

"Brian, just tell them…Tell them. So what? It's out now. No more secrets, no more."

"Officers…Paul, I mean come on, she's obviously losing it—"

"Am I?" I quip turning to look at Deacon Hamilton now. "Deac, I know that you all carry those little portable tests, just test him. I have no reason to lie to you."

Deacon Hamilton just stares at me, unwilling to move, probably out of fear of what he might actually find, but thank God the officers with him weren't.

Within seconds, the stout officer, who seems to be the most outgoing and on point, steps to Brian with a swab test in hand. "Sir, can you please step over here."

"What? Really? I've been kidnapped, beaten, and whatever else and your testing—"

"This way, sir. Thank you." Popping a pen, he flicks Brian from eye to eye. Once he found what he was looking for, he then turns to Hamilton and the other officer. "It's affirmative. His pupils seem to be dilated."

Deacon Hamilton puts his head down but the other officer takes this as his cue to swab him. And within minutes, everyone knows what I knew to be true. Brian bombed the influence test, horribly.

Just to be on the safe side, I guess, the officers tested the rest of us. Every one of us comes up clean.

Embarrassed, Brian still tries to offer up some kind of defense for himself. "Look okay, so I had a little of this and a little of that. That doesn't take away from what happened. I'm the one who's been under attack. You guys are police officers, your job is to protect and serve! Why aren't you doing your ---"

"That'll be enough, Deacon Parker." Hearing Deacon Hamilton drop his voice was a clear indication to Brian that the situation had definitely turned. Handcuffs in hand, Deacon Hamilton moves in to arrest Brian just as the other two officers go off to question Kid and Mike.

"Sir, you have the right to remain silent—"

"Oh, God, really?" he asks now feeling the pressure of the cuffs around his wrists.

". . .can and will be used against you. You have the right to an—"

"Hey, hey, I know my rights. Ole' renter cop—"

". . . if you refuse this—"

"You need to turn in your badge."

"Do you understand your rights, sir?"

"Talking about some officer. You need to go back to the academy and tell them to stop handing out certificates. This ain't April Fools!"

"Alright, that's enough out of you." Just as Hamilton walks out with Brian, in walks Mike and Kid just as free as the day that they were born. I guess it's true, God is the God of second chances. Yeah, I guess He is.

Chapter Six

Kid

Ephesians 3:20 tells us that God can do above all that we can ask or think. Clearly, he's done a lot for me. Brian went down that night but his girl Danielle bailed him out. After his divorce with Trish though, I think that brah just quit trying. Because for all we know, he's been in and out of jail and rehab ever since. And his girl Danielle, well what can I say. She just has this thing for married men. Last I heard, she was trying to get through to the Worship leader, but his wife found out and home girl ain't step foot in another church yet. Mike's still rambling through the streets; he's my uncle and all but he does his own thing now.

And Trish, well she divorced Brian and took the job to rebuild a church in Zimbabwe. She's doing a wonderful job. Not to mention the fact that she got married. Yeah, she's a Harris now and together we're expecting our first child pretty soon. It's a girl and we're going to name her Kenya, just like Trish's mom. Thank God for second chances and I promise you Lord, I'm not going to screw this one up. Until next time, we'll catch up with you all later.

Other Books By Tatiana Whigham

Get Out of the Pews

Do You Know Your Worth?

Lyrics from an Old Soul

From Butterflies to Caterpillars